DISASTER

MW00655062

FREEZE FRAME

SANDRA D. BRICKER

Artesian Press

P.O. Box 355 Buena Park, CA 90621

Take Ten Books
Mystery

Freeze Frame	**1-58659-005-7**
Cassette	**1-58659-010-3**
The Return of the Eagle	1-58659-002-2
Cassette	1-58659-007-3
Touchdown	1-58659-003-0
Cassette	1-58659-008-1
Nobody Lives in Apartment N-2	1-58659-001-4
Cassette	1-58659-006-5
Stick Like Glue	1-58659-004-9
Cassette	1-58659-009-X

Other Take Ten Themes:
Chillers
Sports
Adventure
Disaster
Thrillers
Fantasy

Project Editor: Liz Parker
Cover Illustrator:Marjorie Taylor
Cover Designer: Tony Amaro
Text Illustrator: Fujiko Miller

Artesian Press

ISBN 1-58659-005-7

Chapter 1

Turn—turn—just a little more. Perfect! *Click.* Got it!

A winning photograph waited within the frame of his camera. Bradley Merino was certain of it! He'd spent much of the day shooting photos of children, dogs, joggers, boaters, and anything that looked interesting. He was hoping for a chance at the grand prize in the *Au Naturel* Photo Contest being sponsored by the local newspaper. The prize was a whole new camera set-up. Brad wanted it just as badly as he'd wanted anything that had to do with photography since the time he could hold a camera in his hot little hand.

Everything Brad had done for most of his life was in preparation for a career as a photojournalist. He'd taken lots of photography classes every summer since he was eight years old. The following month when he began his freshman year of high school, he planned to join the Photography Club. Very few boys his age knew what they wanted to do with their lives, but Brad knew. He'd always known. His friends were darting from goal to goal, astronaut to scientist to fireman. But Brad held steady, as focused as that shot of wildflowers within the frame of the viewfinder. *Click.* Good one.

It was the day of the boat race at the lake, and Brad had left home with four rolls of film in his belt. He planned to shoot all 144 exposures, and he was more than three-quarters toward that goal. With just a dozen or so exposures left in the last roll, he headed over to the lake.

The lake looked particularly blue that day—a perfect day for taking pictures! The boat race had given Brad some good action shots. Now that it was over, though, he was looking for something a bit more quiet. The lake looked like glass. The few boats that dotted the surface seemed unreal under the hot, yellow sun.

To the side by the dock, however, things were much different. There seemed to be some sort of uproar. Clumps of people were noisily gathered in a group. Brad reached for his camera around his neck as he moved in closer.

Brad brushed his dark hair away from his face and focused his brown eyes on the scene before him. He knew that the heap beneath the red splotched sheet was a body. Not that he'd ever seen a dead body, but he'd watched enough television to recognize one when he saw it.

He stood back away from the body, brought closer by the zoom lens, and clicked off two or three shots. By the time he lowered the camera from his face, an ambulance had rolled in, and attendants were raising the dead body toward the open doors.

Click. Click. Click. A few more shots, even though the scene was starting to make him feel sick to his stomach. A good photojournalist never thought about his stomach. *Click.* One for good measure.

"Merino!" someone called.

Brad turned to find Victor Neff, a young cop whom he'd met in one of his photography classes the summer before.

"Vic!" Vic was a sight for sore eyes, and Brad moved toward him on shaky legs. "Look at you!"

Brad had seen Vic in his uniform before, but never at the site of a real crime. He looked a lot like the cops on television.

"What are you doing out here today?" Vic asked. Anyone could see what *he* was doing there, with that body in the ambulance in the background.

Click. Brad couldn't resist.

"Now why doesn't that surprise me?" Vic teased. "What else would Kid Photo be doing out on a day like this?"

"What's going on?" Brad asked softly, then nodded toward the ambulance that was backing away.

"A woman was shot out here today," Vic told him. "And nobody even noticed."

"She was shot and no one heard the gun? That's a little unlikely, isn't it?"

"The boat race was already over when she was found. It probably happened while the race was in full swing. Maybe the killer pulled the trigger with the start-off shot. I don't know."

"Who found her?" Brad quizzed.

Vic nodded toward a woman in the arms of her husband. She was crying so hard that the man could hardly hold her to him.

"She spotted her dog eating the woman's picnic lunch and went over to apologize. But the woman was already dead, lying there like she was taking a catnap."

Brad raised his camera and took his last few shots of the crying woman. There was something so real about her, so raw. She was lost in emotion, her own personal tornado, and Brad had managed to capture a little piece of it. Something inside him wriggled a little, as if he had invaded her in some way. But the future photojournalist in him smiled at his triumph. Maybe the *Register* would want to use the photos. Or maybe they would win him that grand prize!

"Have you been shooting all day?" Vic asked as they walked back toward the team of police cars parked at the edge of the park.

"Yes," said Brad, and he rewound the last roll of film through the camera.

"Did you notice anyone? Anybody acting strange?"

"No stranger than usual," Brad grinned.

"Why am I even asking?" Vic joked. "You? Notice anything else when there's a camera in your hand? Forget it!"

"Hey, maybe Kid Photo caught a picture of the murder," one of the cops snickered as they walked past.

"Maybe so," Vic said without turning around, then he rolled his eyes for only Brad to see. "Want a ride home?"

"Nah," answered Brad as he continued on through the crowd of onlookers surrounding the police cars. "See you later."

Chapter 2

He didn't know why, but Brad found himself circling the park and coming right back to where he had first seen the body, covered with the white sheet, motionless and dead.

He didn't know why he had wandered back to that spot, or why it interested him, but he couldn't seem to shake the memory of it. Perhaps it was the shock of it. Or perhaps it had been that quick view of soft, white skin of the dead woman's hand where it hung over the side of the stretcher.

Brad could watch anyone on television being blown away in bloody fits of violence and never even get scared. But somehow he knew this one dead woman might haunt him for the rest of his life. It was real. Too real. Someone had actually been murdered, and Brad had been close enough to the body to photograph it. It sent an eerie chill straight through him.

He headed up the hill toward the bike stand at the edge of the parking lot. There weren't many people still around. The race was over, and the murder had sent hundreds of people home to lock their doors behind them, flip on the television, and forget what they'd seen.

Brad bent down to struggle with the lock on his bike chain, as always. He just had to remember to get a new lock. Before that thought left his mind, he was struck hard in the back of the head. He was on the ground before he could even think.

"What the . . .?"

As he looked up at the attacker, a large fist landed right beneath his eye, and Brad fell backward to the ground. The huge hands turned him over and shoved his face hard into the concrete. He felt as if his nose might be broken. When he lifted his head he saw his own blood streaming down upon the pavement. He hardly felt the camera being lifted over his head until the strap tore several locks of hair from his scalp.

"Geeeeez!" he screamed, and the pain caused him to fall back to the ground, face first.

Brad could hear his attacker running away, but he couldn't manage to look up after him. Blood was everywhere, and the pain was nearly enough to make him unconscious. It was several moments before Brad could even sit up. In another half hour he unhitched his bike and headed home, nothing but his accessory belt and three rolls of film around his waist.

Brad knew he would have to report

the crime tomorrow. He wondered if the police could find the guy without a description. He was in too much pain to think about having lost his camera, but the reality hit him hard that night. He didn't get much sleep.

Chapter 3

Four days had healed a lot of Brad's face, but hadn't healed his pride. He stood before the bathroom mirror and looked at himself with anger.

"Wimp," he said aloud. "Some guy comes along and takes your camera, and what do you do? You let him!"

"Bradley, are you all right?" his mother called from the hall.

"Fine, Mom." Why was she always so close by?

The bruise over his eye was just beginning to lose a bit of its shine. The cuts across his nose and lips were healing, but sore. He didn't feel much like riding into town that day, but he wanted to pick up the three rolls of prints he had left at the film developer. The photographs he'd taken at the scene of the murder had been in the stolen camera, but maybe a winning shot was somewhere in the other three rolls. The *Au Naturel* grand prize was his only hope at replacing his lost camera outfit before the start of the school year, just three weeks away. No camera, no Photography Club. It just wasn't fair.

Brad couldn't even wait to go back home before looking at the prints. He ran across the street from the developer to the diner, ordered a vanilla soda, and began sorting through the shots. The reject pile was overflowing. Only four or five made it from each of the three packets into the maybe pile. None of them was as good as what he'd shot at the scene of the murder, and Brad flung himself back into the booth in anger.

"What's the matter, Bradley?"

Connie, the waitress, asked in concern.

"Nothin'." He just didn't feel much like conversation.

"Okay," she sighed, and she set the vanilla soda on the table and walked away.

Brad leaned forward and began looking through the photographs again. One of the best was a side shot down a row of people at the edge of the lake. He had taken it during the boat race, and the faces were filled with excitement. That could be a winner. There was no use comparing it to the shots that were stolen with his camera and zoom lens.

"Just look at what you have here," he groaned to himself. "Just look at what you have."

This one wasn't bad. And this one. And this one was pretty great. A little girl, nose-to-nose with a huge Sheepdog. Brad wondered if that was the dog who had been eating the dead woman's

picnic.

"Stop it!" he ordered himself. "Just get her out of your mind!"

"Oh," Connie cooed above him. "Girl troubles?"

"No, Connie. What do you want?"

"Can I get you a refill?"

"No."

He knew he was being rude, but he just wanted to be left alone! Connie must have taken the hint, because, when he looked up to apologize for his gruffness, she was gone.

Brad reached for the glass and took one last gulp from it. Then he took two huge pieces of ice into his mouth and began to crunch them between his teeth. He liked the way the cold felt inside his mouth. It helped him think. Some people tapped their fingers, others chewed on the ends of their pens. Brad crunched ice.

It wasn't until he began clearing the table and placing the photographs back in their packets that he saw it. Brad stopped mid-crunch, as frozen as the block of ice between his teeth. He strained to get a clearer look.

"Huh ...?" He held the photograph up close to his face. He squinted. Could it be?

In the background of the shot, beyond the curly-haired child and the wild-haired Sheepdog, Brad could almost see it. A man, he thought, was behind the tree. Clearly, a hand. Holding something. The handle was oddly discolored, but it was absolutely ... he could almost be positive ... a gun!

Brad gasped for breath through his excitement. "A gun," he muttered. "A gun!"

"Again?" Connie called from behind the counter. "Refill again?"

"No," he chuckled nervously. "No, thanks. No more for me."

It took less than thirty seconds for Brad to gather up his things and toss two dollars at Connie across the counter.

"Keep the change," he called as he raced out the door into the street.

He couldn't make it across the street fast enough. He burst through the doors of the photo shop like some sort of explosion.

"Back so soon?" the man asked him.

"Yes," he mumbled as he flicked through the negatives one strip at a time. "Here it is! Here. I need an enlargement of this one. The one of the little girl and the dog."

"Five by seven? Eight by ten?" the man offered.

"Let's say sixteen by twenty!" Brad said in a loud, excited voice. "How soon can I get this?"

"One week," he answered, already writing out the order.

"A week? I can't ... it can't wait that long. Isn't there some way to get it sooner?"

"Well, now, that would cost you."

"I don't care!" Brad blurted. "I just need it quickly."

"Rush service then," the man stated. "Three working days."

Chapter 4

Three days seemed like forever to Brad. He would fill the time finding out as much about the murdered woman as he could. She rose up in his mind once again at the thought of helping solve her murder.

A visit to the library revealed that Stacie Minors was 28 years old, an artist, new in town. When she'd arrived earlier that year, she'd taken a job at the Lakeside Art Gallery answering phones and doing some sales work. That same gallery had planned an exhibit of her work in the fall.

Brad was still thinking about all that he had learned as he walked into the police station at the top of the hill. He wanted to find Vic and tell him about the photograph, even though it wouldn't be ready until the following day. But Vic was nowhere to be found. As usual, he was out on his beat, doing his policeman thing.

Brad paused to look at a photograph among many on the wall. It was Vic, being presented with a special award by the mayor. Brad didn't remember the occasion and figured it must have happened before they met last year.

He wore that same bright smile Brad had come to know so well, and Brad smiled back at the photograph. Vic was a good-looking man, with shiny, sandy hair. His green eyes glistened, even in the black and white photo. He was muscular and strong, very strong, and in better shape than most of the other cops on the force. There was fifteen years between them, but Brad considered Vic a friend.

Maybe his best friend, since there weren't too many others to compare him to. Older friends were better anyway. They didn't go to the same school. They didn't know if you were a nerd.

Chapter 5

The larger photo proved Brad's theory beyond any doubt. The hand was holding a gun. A special gun, too. The gun definitely had an ivory or pearl handle.

So many thoughts ran through Brad's mind all at once. He remembered that girl's body beneath the bloody sheet at the park. For the first time, he found himself wondering about her family, about her friends. Did she have a boyfriend? He imagined how he would have felt if he were Stacie Minors' boyfriend and heard the news of her death.

Brad had never lost anyone to death, and he thought for the first time that he might know what it felt like. In his way, he did know Stacie Minors. He knew her through her love of her art. He had the same love for photography. He promised himself that he would go to her show at the gallery in the fall. Something inside of him felt connected to her, and he wanted to do that for her. He might even buy something and hang it on his wall in her memory. In memory of her life, or life in general. A reminder of how quickly life can be needlessly snatched away.

Brad ran all the way to the police station, tucking the photograph inside his jacket as he ran. By the time he reached the top of the hill, he was breathless. He found himself wishing he had called ahead. Vic was never at the station, he remembered. Today was no different.

"Vic? Is he around?" Brad gasped at the man behind the front desk.

"No," he responded as Brad expected, "out on a case."

"Ugggh," he groaned, catching his breath. "Can I leave him a note?"

"Sure, go ahead."

Brad made his way around the desk and hopped the gate without opening it. His Reeboks squeaked on the floor as he hurried toward Vic's desk. He sat down and rested in the chair for a minute before searching through the drawers to find some paper.

Brad noticed that Commissioner Barnes was being interviewed inside his office. Several reporters were gathered around him. Brad figured it must be about that unsolved murder in the park the day of the boat race. Brad smiled to himself. Wouldn't they be surprised when he showed them the photo with the gun!

For a moment, he dreamed about popping into the Commissioner's office with the photograph and telling his story. He imagined those cameras flashing in his face and the reporters calling in their stories, covering the microphones as they asked for the spelling of the hero's name.

"Merino. M-E-R-I-N-O."

He shook the thoughts from his head. He wanted to talk to Vic first. They would decide the best way to handle it.

He quickly scribbled a note: "Vic: Urgent that we talk." With a second thought, he added, "No kidding. Urgent. Brad."

Brad noticed that Commissioner Barnes looked calm and cool handling the reporters' questions. He moved in closer to listen. Brad noticed another batch of framed photographs on the wall over Barnes' shoulder. He stared at one of them in particular.

In the photo, the Commissioner stood over a huge cake that read, "25 Years of Service." He was shaking hands with the Mayor. No, they

weren't shaking hands. The Mayor was presenting him with a very special handgun. The handle was made of pearl, and a tiny gold badge was engraved on the side.

Brad felt his heart flop over inside his chest. He stepped forward to look more closely at the photograph. There was no escaping it. Even though he knew how foolish it would be, he wanted to pull the photo from his pocket to compare that gun with the Commissioner's.

The Commissioner.

Brad looked up just in time for his eyes to meet Commissioner Barnes' eyes. His pulse raced through his body, and he felt dizzy. He didn't know what to do, but he felt the threat in the eyes of the Police Commissioner.

"To protect and to serve." It was written on a sign in the commissioner's office. There would be no protection for Brad from this policeman, Brad knew that for sure!

Barnes watched closely as Brad turned and ran from the station house. Coolly, Barnes dismissed the reporters and walked out of his office.

He called to the guy behind the front desk and smiled. "Who was that kid looking for?"

"Vic Neff, sir," the officer answered.

Chapter 6

Brad ran all the way to Vic's house in the woods by the lake, shouting Vic's name before he ever made it to the door.

"Victor?!"

Brad pounded his fist against the door. Then he moved around to the window and peered inside.

"Vic?"

Brad's mind was racing, putting all of the facts together, trying desperately to make sense out of it all. Why would the Commissioner have killed that girl? And why didn't any of the cops see him that day at the lake? Was the Commissioner the one who stole his camera that day? The way he had looked at

Brad through his office window brought a chill up and down Brad's spine. The Commissioner would be looking for him. And if he found the note he left for Vic, he might be right on his trail.

Brad quickly ran toward the edge of the nearby woods. He carefully camouflaged himself in the bushes and decided to wait there for Vic to come home. If Barnes showed up in the meantime, he surely wouldn't notice Brad there.

Another hour passed before there was any movement around Brad besides a slight breeze and his own raging thoughts. Finally Vic's Jeep came rolling down the gravel hill toward the house. Brad waited until Vic parked the car. Then he emerged from the woods and raced to Vic's side.

"Merino. What are you doing here?"

"Vic, I've got the most incredible piece of evidence for you," Brad began.

"You just won't believe what I found out about Stacie Minors' murder."

Vic interrupted. "What kind of evidence? You want to be a cop now?"

"Just listen to me, will you, Vic? I have a photograph here."

He pulled the photo from his jacket and showed it to Vic. Vic motioned for Brad to follow him. Once they were inside, Brad told the story so fast that Vic couldn't actually keep up. The photo. The gun. The Commissioner.

"Commissioner Barnes?" questioned Vic in a high pitch. "Come on, Merino."

"Vic, I'm sure about this. Just look at the gun in this photograph! It was taken at the lake the day of Stacie Minors' murder."

"Oh, my God," Vic whispered. "This is unbelievable."

"Give me the photograph, son."

Vic and Brad spun around to find Commissioner Barnes standing in the doorway, his very special .38 pointed right at them.

"Commissioner," Vic sighed. "Is this true?"

"Give me the photograph," he repeated sternly.

After a long moment of thought, Vic turned to Brad. "Hand it over to him, Brad."

"What?"

"Do as he says."

"No way!" Brad insisted. "No way. How can you say that?"

"He's thinking clearly," Barnes explained. "Like a good cop. He doesn't want to see you get hurt."

"Vic, it's the only evidence you have!"

"Tell him again, Neff," the Commissioner said softly. "Hand it over."

"Forget it!" Brad snapped.

But Vic grabbed the photograph out of Brad's hand and headed slowly for Barnes. "Let the boy go," Vic said as he neared the Commissioner.

"The photograph," Barnes half-grinned.

"Vic, don't give it to him," Brad cried. "Don't give it to him."

Chapter 7

Brad realized that Vic was going to hand over the photograph. He jumped out toward him and snatched it away. Without a moment's warning, Barnes' gun went off, putting a bullet into Brad's left arm. Vic threw several punches, the last of which knocked Barnes' gun from his hand.

Vic and Barnes faced each other breathlessly, both of them eyeing the gun off to the side between them.

"Don't do it, sir," Vic warned him. "Don't go for it."

"You know I have to, Neff," Barnes answered, but neither of them moved.

"I can get it, Vic," Brad groaned from the corner of the room, blood on his fingers where he clutched his wounded arm.

"Don't move, Bradley," Vic instructed him. "Don't move."

Brad waited several long moments, trembling now with the pain of being shot.

"Why did you do it?" Vic asked Barnes. "Why did you kill the girl? Were you involved with her?"

Barnes laughed. "Yes. Involved."

"Surely there was another way to ..."

"No, no," Barnes groaned. "There was no other way. Stacie threatened to tell my wife Ruby the whole truth about our affair. Ruby would have left me, that was for sure. I couldn't risk losing her."

"Sir, you risked that by being involved with another woman," Vic said softly, honestly trying to understand.

"It was a harmless affair," Barnes said.

Brad wanted to tell him there was no such thing as a harmless affair. Someone always got hurt. Even at his age he knew that! But he changed his mind and remained quiet.

"I thought if I could just get rid of Stacie," he continued. "But she wouldn't leave town. She just wouldn't. And there she was on the blanket beside me, just lying there, her eyes closed. It was so simple."

"So you timed your shot with the start-off shot of the race," Vic said.

"Yes," he admitted. "No one ever even noticed. I just got up and walked away, and no one ever even noticed!"

"Neff," Barnes pleaded. "I'm desperate. I'll lose everything if you don't help me."

"He's not going to help you!" Brad shouted from the corner.

"Let's get rid of the boy, Neff," he continued. "And the photograph. I'm your superior officer, Neff. Help me. I order you to help me. I can reward you well."

Vic looked at Barnes seriously. "I'm not going to cover for you, sir. You've murdered a young woman."

"Why not make it three then?" Barnes snickered. "Why not? I'll kill you two as well."

He took one step forward. Vic motioned him to stop with his hand. "Don't, sir. Please."

Barnes stopped in his tracks and thought for a moment. With a sudden turn, he headed for the door and ran out. Vic and Brad were after him immediately. They both landed on Barnes with a thud, and the three of them rolled off the porch into the dirt.

Brad's arm throbbed with pain as he twisted the Commissioner over on his side and shoved him down, face first, into the dirt.

"Taste that dirt?" he said right into Barnes' ear. "Just like you made me taste it the day you stole my camera."

Vic slapped a pair of handcuffs around Barnes' wrists.

"Call the station," Vic ordered Brad, then turned back to Barnes. "Sir, you have the right to remain silent ..."

Brad spoke along with Vic as he headed inside to the phone. "You have the right to an attorney. If you can't afford one, the court will appoint one for you.... Yes, Officer? This is Bradley Merino. I'm calling for Officer Neff. I'm out at his place. We need some help out here...."

Chapter 8

Boats were sailing across the lake in all directions, and the bold golds and reds of fall gave Brad a perfect background for the sailboats through his camera's viewfinder.

One slight turn to bring it sharply into focus and—*click.*

"Good," Brad said aloud as he lowered his camera.

He took a quick glance at his camera. Just about the best camera around. The camera was the grand prize in the *Register's* photo contest, and Brad had won it with his photograph of the little girl and the dog, with the very special background. A huge write-up in the *Register* and the grand prize won him the position of president of the Photography Club at school. And today was the most special day of all.

"Merino!" Vic called from a few yards behind him. "It's almost time."

Brad waved and headed back. As he approached the platform near the entrance of the Lakeside Gallery, a crowd of people clapped.

He was a little embarrassed by the attention, but he smiled and took the steps up the side of the stage. He looked at all of the people and to the side of the crowd where Stacie Minors' paintings were displayed.

"Today, we honor Stacie Minors, a very special local artist," the man at the podium said into the microphone. "And we honor the young man who caught her killer. He's a local artist also. The winner of the *Au Naturel* photo contest, and the winner of the mayor's Special Service Award—Bradley Merino."

Brad stepped forward to the stand

to the clapping and hoots and hollers, and he smiled down at all of them. His parents seemed so proud, and Vic looked as if he were about to pop, clapping and whistling, beaming that big old smile of his. Behind them, Brad caught sight of the photograph of Stacie Minors that was displayed with her work. He couldn't help smiling at her, too.

"Thank you, all of you," he said almost shyly. "I remember the day that Stacie Minors was killed, the day I saw them taking away her body under a blood-stained sheet. I'll never forget that day. It was the day I learned how precious life is. It was the day I decided to make every moment count and to enjoy every moment I have."

He paused to the quiet attention of hundreds of people.

"I accept these awards for every artist like Stacie, and like me," he continued. "For everyone whose art will live on long after they're gone."

He reached beneath the stand and pulled out a canvas, a lively, colorful painting of the lake behind them, and he held it up to the people gathered at the foot of the stage.

"This is the last painting that Stacie completed before her death. Stacie Minors lives through her art," Brad said softly into the microphone. "She lives on in everyone who knew her, and she lives on in my heart."